1, 2,

Buckle My Shoe

1, 2,
Buckle My Shoe

Liz Loveless

Hyperion Books for Children
New York

First published in 1993 by ABC, All Books for Children,

a division of The All Children's Company Ltd.,

33 Museum Street, London WC1A 1LD, United Kingdom.

First published in the USA by Hyperion Books for Children,

114 Fifth Avenue, New York, NY 10011.

FIRST EDITION

1 3 5 7 9 10 8 6 4 2

Library of Congress Cataloging-in-Publication Data

Loveless, Liz.

1, 2, buckle my shoe/Liz Loveless.

p.   cm.

Summary: An illustrated version of the traditional counting rhyme.

ISBN 1-56282-477-5 — ISBN 1-56282-478-3 (lib. bdg.)

1. Nursery rhymes. 2. Children's poetry. [1. Nursery rhymes.

2. Counting.] I. Title. II. Title: One, two, buckle my shoe.

PZ8.3.L934Ab   1993

[E] — dc20   92-40947

CIP

AC

For
Jessie & Lily
& Rurah

1, 2,

Buckle my shoe.

3, 4,

Knock at the door.

5, 6,

Pick up sticks.

7,   8,

Lay them straight.

9, 10,

A big fat hen.

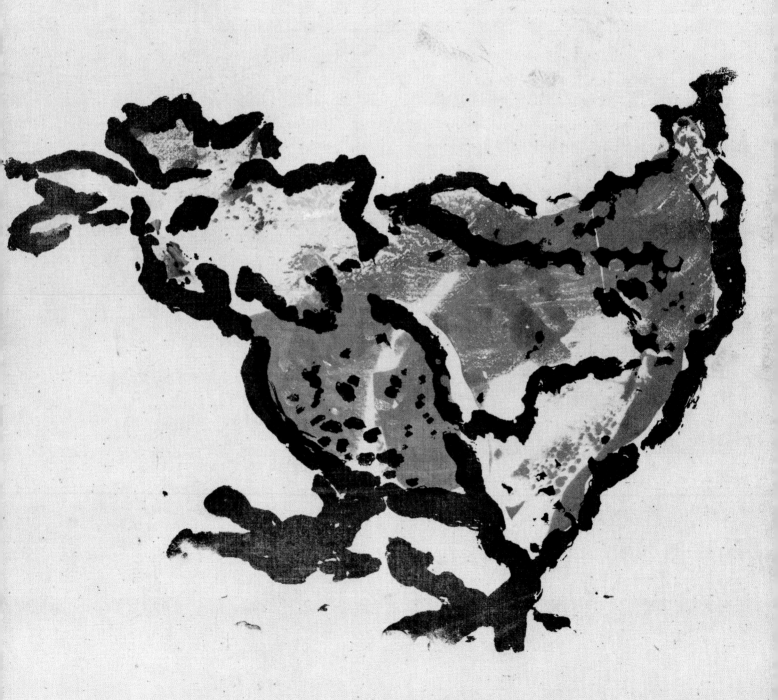

11, 12,

Dig and delve.

13,   14,

Maids a-courting.

15, 16,

Maids a-kissing.

17, 18,

Maids a-waiting.

19, 20,

My plate's empty.